FOR THE TRIXTER,
MY OWN LITTLE MONSTER

Printed in Malaysia

First Edition, September 2005

20 19 18 17 16 15 14 13 12 11

FAC-029191-18020

Library of Congress Cataloging-in-Publication Data on file.

ISBN 978-0-7868-5294-9

Reinforced binding

Visit www.hyperionbooksforchildren.com
and www.pigeonpresents.com

YOUR PAL MO WILLEMS PRESENTS

Leonardo

the

TERRIBLE

MONSTER

HYPERION BOOKS FOR CHILDREN/NEW YORK

LEONARDO

WAS A

TERRIBLE

MONSTER...

HE COULDN'T SCARE ANYONE.

HE DIDN'T HAVE 1,642* TEETH, LIKE TONY.

*NOTE: NOT ALL TEETH SHOWN.

HE
WASN'T
BIG,
LIKE
ELEANOR.

AND HE WASN'T
JUST PLAIN WEIRD,
LIKE HECTOR.

LEONARDO TRIED VERY HARD TO BE SCARY.

BUT...

HE JUST WASN'T.

ONE DAY,
LEONARDO HAD AN IDEA.
HE WOULD FIND THE MOST
SCAREDY-CAT KID IN
THE WHOLE WORLD...

AND SCARE THE TUNA SALAD OUT OF HIM!

LEONARDO RESEARCHED

UNTIL HE FOUND THE PERFECT CANDIDATE...

SAM.

LEONARDO SNUCK UP
ON THE POOR,
UNSUSPECTING
BOY.

UNTIL
THE LITTLE BOY
CRIED.

AND THE
MONSTER GAVE IT
ALL HE HAD.

"NO YOU DIDN'T!" SNAPPED SAM.

"YES!" CHEERED LEONARDO. "I DID IT! I'VE FINALLY SCARED THE TUNA SALAD OUT OF SOMEONE!"

"OH, YEAH?" REPLIED LEONARDO. "THEN WHY ARE YOU CRYING?"

"MY MEAN BIG BROTHER STOLE OF MY HANDS WHILE I WAS STILL BROKE IT ON PURPOSE, AND IT TRIED TO FIX IT BUT I COULDN'T, TABLE AND I STUBBED MY TOE LAST MONTH WHEN I ACCIDENTALLY I GOT SOAP IN MY EYES TRYING TO THAT MY BROTHER'S COCKATOO DON'T HAVE ANY FRIENDS AND

MY ACTION FIGURE RIGHT OUT PLAYING WITH IT, AND THEN HE WAS MY FAVORITE TOY, AND I AND I GOT SO MAD I KICKED THE ON THE SAME FOOT THAT I HURT SLIPPED IN THE BATHTUB AFTER WASH OUT THE BIRD POO POOPED ON MY HEAD AND I MY TUMMY HURTS!"

THEN
LEONARDO
MADE

A VERY BIG DECISION.

INSTEAD OF BEING
A TERRIBLE MONSTER,
HE WOULD BECOME
A WONDERFUL FRIEND.

(BUT THAT DIDN'T MEAN
THAT HE COULDN'T TRY
TO SCARE HIS FRIEND
EVERY NOW AND THEN!)

THE END